Little Whistle's Dinner Party

CYNTHIA RYLANT

Illustrated by TIM BOWERS

Harcourt, Inc.

San Diego   New York   London

For Margaret

—C. R.

To Glenn, Esther, Aumaine, and Haans

—T. B.

Text copyright © 2001 by Cynthia Rylant
Illustrations copyright © 2001 by Tim Bowers

www.harcourt.com

Library of Congress Cataloging-in-Publication Data
Rylant, Cynthia.
Little Whistle's dinner party/Cynthia Rylant; illustrated by Tim Bowers.
p.   cm.
Summary: A guinea pig who lives in Toytown invites his friends
in the toy store to a dinner party at midnight.
[1. Guinea pigs—Fiction. 2. Toys—Fiction. 3. Parties—Fiction.]
I. Bowers, Tim, ill. II. Title.
PZ7.R982Li   2001
[E]—dc21   99-12383
ISBN 0-15-201079-3

First edition
H G F E D C B A

Printed in Singapore

The illustrations in this book were done in oil paint on canvas.
The display type was set in Minister Light.
The text type was set in Goudy Catalogue.
Color separations by Bright Arts Ltd., Hong Kong
Printed and bound by Tien Wah Press, Singapore
This book was printed on totally chlorine-free Nymolla Matte Art paper.
Production supervision by Sandra Grebenar and Ginger Boyer
Designed by Lydia D'moch

Toytown was home to many wonderful toys and to one small guinea pig named Little Whistle.

Little Whistle did not mind being the only live thing in Toytown. He slept all day while children looked at toys and at him in his cozy cage. Then at night, when all the people were gone and the shades drawn, Little Whistle woke up to start a new adventure.

Toytown was a perfect place for adventure because after the shades were drawn, the toys blinked their eyes and moved their heads and stopped acting like toys altogether. Little Whistle knew many of them by name, and each evening he traveled through the store, visiting old friends.

One particular night, Little Whistle woke up feeling quite hungry. He put on his blue pea coat and took the train to see Bear at the other end of the store.

Bear was trying on a fireman's helmet when Little Whistle arrived.

"Hello, Bear," said Little Whistle with a smile. "Have you eaten?"

Bear set down the helmet and picked up a baseball cap.

"Why no," said Bear. "I've been so busy with hats."

"I am thinking of having a dinner party," said Little Whistle. "Can you come at midnight?"

"Certainly!" said Bear. "I shall wear my fedora."

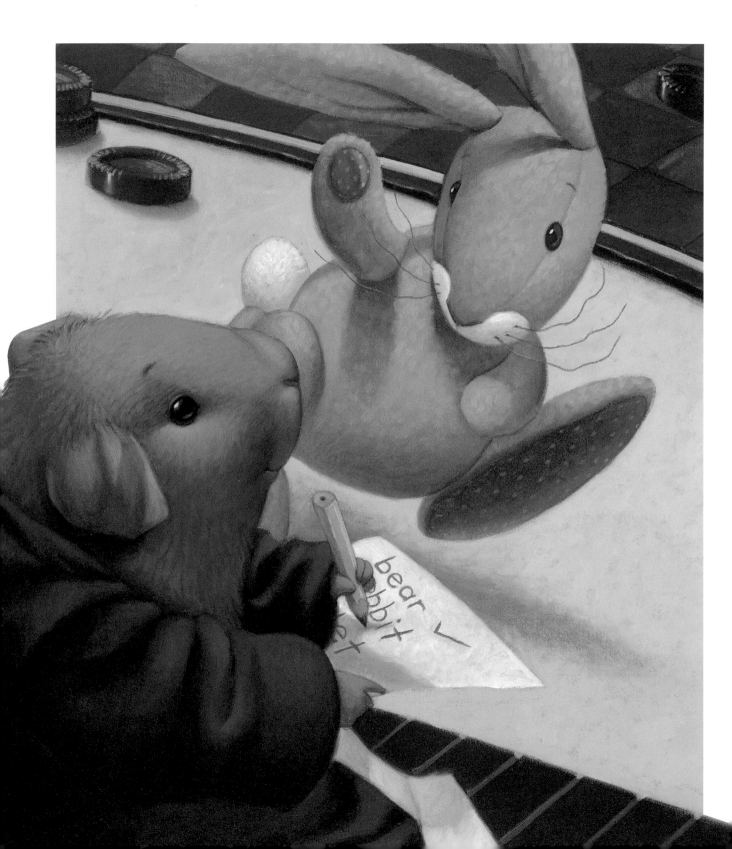

Little Whistle rode the train all over the store, inviting his friends to dinner.

"I'll run right over!" said Rabbit, who always ran after the shades were drawn.

"I'll bring a smile and a song!" said Violet, the little china doll who liked to sing.

"Will there be any vanilla cookies?" asked Lion, who loved them. "Try to have vanilla cookies!"

Soldier gave Little Whistle a sharp salute and said, "Once the babies are asleep, I'll march right over!" (Each night, Soldier read stories to all the Toytown babies.)

When Little Whistle had finished inviting all of his friends, it was time to put together dinner.

He walked down a long aisle lined with tiny ovens and silver kettles and china tea sets.

He opened an oven door and looked inside.

"Perfect!" he said. He put the oven into a little shopping cart and moved on.

Next he chose a lovely blue willow tea set and a sturdy whistling kettle. Then he rolled everything back to his cage.

Inside the cage was a special corner where Little Whistle kept hidden all of his best guinea pig treats. He kept them for special occasions like this one.

So into the tiny oven he put four shiny brown chestnuts, a small red potato, three spears of asparagus, and a breadstick to bake.

Little Whistle's cage was too small for company, so while dinner was baking, he cleared the Toytown counter and spread it with the lovely blue willow dishes. He filled the shiny kettle at the watercooler and set it on top of the stove for tea.

Then he went in search of dessert.

At midnight Little Whistle's guests began arriving. Bear looked very handsome in his fedora. He had brought along a mirror so he could admire his hat during dinner. Violet came singing and smiling. Soldier marched to the party with a book under his arm. Lion showed up looking very hungry. And, of course, Rabbit ran by several times before finally stopping.

But where was Little Whistle?

He was coming in a helicopter! All of the dinner guests waved as Little Whistle traveled toward them. And what was he holding? A box of vanilla cookies!

It was a wonderful dinner party. And afterward everyone had tea and vanilla cookies. (Lion was very happy.)

Naturally, the helicopter pilot took a nice plate of food home. It was the least Little Whistle could do, as thanks for a lift to the all-night grocery!

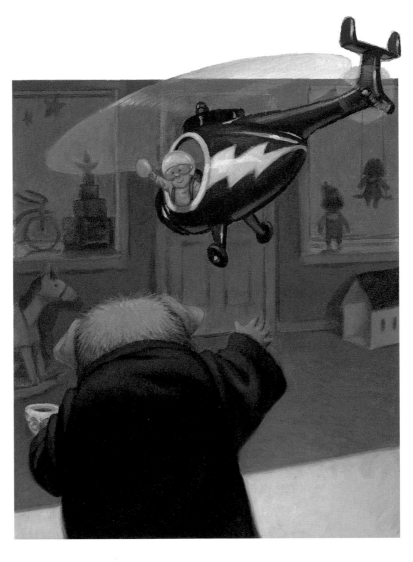